ZONDERKIDZ

The Berenstain Bears® God Shows the Way
Copyright © 2014 by Berenstain Publishing, Inc.
Illustrations © 2014 by Berenstain Publishing, Inc.

Requests for information should be addressed to:
Zonderkidz, 3900 *Sparks Dr, Grand Rapids, Michigan 49546*
ISBN 978-0-310-74211-1

Faith Gets Us Through ISBN 9780310725015
Do Not Fear, God Is Near ISBN 9780310725114
Piggy Bank Blessings ISBN 9780310725053

Editor: Mary Hassinger
Design: Diane Mielke

Printed in China

15 16 17 18 19 /DSC/ 10 9 8 7 6 5 4

Even though I walk
through the darkest valley,
I will fear no evil,
for you are with me.

—Psalm 23:4

ZONDERkidz I Can Read!™

BEGINNING 1 READING

The Berenstain Bears®
Faith Gets Us Through

Story and Pictures By
Stan & Jan Berenstain with Mike Berenstain

Living Lights™

Today was a special day.

The Bear Scouts were going to

Spooky Cave.

They wanted to earn their

Cave Adventure Merit Badges.

Scout Sister said, "I am a little scared."

Scout Brother said, "Me, too."

Scout Fred said, "As the Bible says,
'The Lord is my light and my salvation
—whom shall I fear?'"

Spooky Cave looked spooky!

It looked like a big, open mouth

with big, sharp teeth.

Scout Papa said, "Come on, scouts.

Don't be scared.

All we need is a little faith.

Let's earn those badges."

Mountain goats watched Papa

and the scouts go into the cave.

Scouts Papa, Brother, Sister, and Fred
went in Spooky Cave.

Papa said, "If you have a question,
just ask me.

I know all about caves."

Sister asked,

"What are these pointy things?"

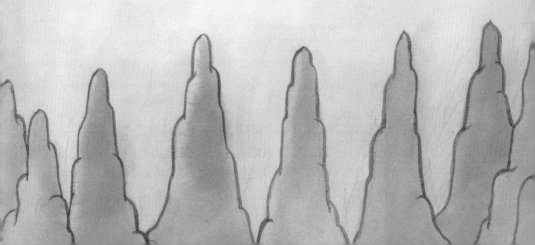

Fred said,
"Some of those pointy
things grow up and
some grow down."

Papa said, "Yes. Listen to this rhyme—
Stalactites and stalagmites,
Only caves got 'em.
Tites are up on top.
Mites are on the bottom."

The scouts looked up.

They looked down.

God made amazing things!

Then Sister said,

"It sounds funny in the cave."

Papa said, "I know all about caves,

so let me tell you.

It sounds funny because there is an

echo in the cave.

Listen."

Papa shouted, "HELLO!"

The scouts heard the sound bounce

off the cave walls.

'HELLO! Hello! Hello!'

went the echo.

But Papa forgot that noises in
a cave can shake things loose.

"Be strong and courageous,"
Fred quoted from the Bible.
"And look out!"

"YIPE!" said Papa.

A falling stalactite just missed him!

Papa and the scouts went
deeper into the cave.
The scouts said a prayer to
keep up their courage.

Soon, they could not
remember which
way they had
come.

Sister asked, "Are we lost?"

Papa said, "We are not lost.

I know all about caves so

I left a trail of string."

But Papa did not know a goat

had followed them.

The goat had eaten the trail of string.

The scouts asked, "What will we do?"

Papa said, "Never fear!

I know all about caves."

Papa got his finger wet. He held it up.

"I feel a breeze," said Papa.

"That means there is another way out."

But Papa did not know about

the stream in Spooky Cave.

"Yiiieee!" shouted Papa, as he fell in the water.

"Lord, help us!" prayed the scouts.

Down,

down

they went.

Down,

down,

down …

… and out of

Spooky Cave.

God kept them safe.
The scouts were
back outside!

Papa said, "Here are your Cave
Adventure Merit Badges."

Fred said, "Our faith and prayers
sure helped us get through."
Sister said, "It was fun."
Brother said, "Just like a water slide."

"Scout Papa, may we go back

in the cave?" Fred asked.

Papa said, "Scouts, I know all about caves.

I am glad you asked that question.

The answer is …

But the scouts were happy.

They were happy they had faith.

They were happy they had their badges.

They were happy Papa knew
everything about caves.

Well ...

almost everything.

I sought the Lord, and he answered me; he delivered me from all my fears.

—Psalm 34:4

The Berenstain Bears.
Do Not Fear, God is Near

Story and Pictures By
Stan & Jan Berenstain with Mike Berenstain

Living Lights™

When Sister Bear was little
she was afraid of lots of things.

She was afraid of bugs.

She was afraid of birds.

She was afraid of dogs

and thunder and
lightning.

But Sister was most afraid

of spooky shadows.

When Sister got bigger
she understood that trust in God
takes away our fears.

As the Bible says:

"When I am afraid, I put my trust in you.

In God, whose word I praise—

in God I trust and am not afraid."

She was not even afraid
of thunder and lightning!

But Sister was still afraid of
spooky shadows.

"You know, Sister," Mama told her,
"God is always near you,
even when things seem scary."

Brother Bear thought Sister was silly.

He teased her.

"Scaredy bear! Scaredy bear!

Afraid of your own shadow,"

Brother teased.

It was not nice.

But big brothers are not always

nice to little sisters—even Brother Bear.

"That is not nice," said Mama.

"You should be kind to your sister.

As the Good Book says,
'Anyone who withholds kindness
from a friend forsakes the fear
of the Almighty.'"
"That is right," said Papa.
"Besides, Sister is brave about
many other things."

Sister was not afraid of frogs and toads.

She was not afraid of spooky-shaped trees.

And one day when a big spider came and sat beside her ...

Sister scared the spider away.

But Sister was still scared

of shadows.

She forgot that the Bible says,

"Do not be afraid or discouraged,

for the Lord God, my God, is with you."

"Help!" Sister cried.

"Spooky shadows!"

Sister ran into the tree house

and into Papa's arms.

"We must do something,"
said Mama.

"I have an idea," said Papa.

"Look, Sister," Papa said.

"Shadows can be fun."

He gave her a flashlight
to shine on the wall.

Then Papa made a funny

shadow.

"It looks like a bird,"
said Sister.

Sister looked at Papa's hands.

She looked at the shadow.

Papa wiggled his hands.

The bird flapped its wings.

"It is flapping its wings!" said Sister.

"May I try?"

Papa held the flashlight.

Sister made a bird shadow too.

"You see," said Papa, "a shadow is what happens when something gets in the way of a light."

Then Papa showed Sister
how to make a shadow rabbit,

a shadow goose,

and a shadow dog.

Later that night, Sister played

a trick on Brother.

She made a big shadow bird
and flapped its wings.

"Yipe!" Brother cried.
"A spooky shadow!"

Sister knew she should not tease.
But she wanted to teach
Brother a little lesson.

When they were in bed,

Sister knew she should be kind to Brother.

But she teased him

one more time.

She made a rabbit,

a goose, and a dog.

"Spooky shadows!"

Brother cried.

Papa came in.

"You should not tease your brother,"
he said.

"But I see you are not afraid
of shadows anymore."

"I guess not,"
Sister said.

But Brother was—a little.

Then he remembered that God

was watching over him.

As the Book of Proverbs says,

"When you lie down, you will not be afraid;

When you lie down, your sleep will be sweet."

Whoever gathers money little by
little makes it grow.

—*Proverbs 13:11*

I Can Read!™

BEGINNING
1
READING

The Berenstain Bears®
PIGGY BANK
BLESSINGS

Story and Pictures By

Stan & Jan Berenstain with Mike Berenstain

Living
Lights™

Brother and Sister Bear liked shopping
with Mama.

One day, Brother saw a toy he wanted.

Brother said, "May I have that toy plane?"

Mama said, "Yes."

Sister saw a teddy bear.

Sister said, "May I have that teddy?"

Mama said, "Yes."

But Mama did not say yes all the time.

"I want that truck too,"
Brother said.

Mama said, "No, not today."

"Why not?" asked Brother.

"You cannot have all the things
you want," said Mama.

"Why?" asked Sister.

Then Mama had an idea.

Mama bought a bank.

She said, "I will teach you

about money."

The new bank looked like a small pig.

It had a slot for money.

"The Bible says we should all

set aside some money.

This will help you save,"

Mama said.

Mama told the cubs about

saving money for something special.

She told them when they got money

as gifts it should go in the bank.

Sometimes
they got pennies.

Sometimes
they got nickels …

or dimes …

or quarters.

And sometimes
they got dollar bills!

Brother and Sister got money

for the jobs they did.

They emptied trash.

They watered flowers.

They pulled weeds.

Mama had told them
they should save for
something special.
And that is just what
the cubs did.

One day Mama said, "You cubs
are doing a good job saving."
"Thank you," said Sister.
"But when we want to use it for
something special, how will we
get the money out?"
Mama said, "You will know
when the time comes."

Then one day, Brother and Sister
knew the time had come.
They needed the money for
something special.
Sister said, "Now how do we
get the money out?"

"There's only one way
to do it," Brother said.

He got his toy hammer.

CRASH went the piggy bank.

The money spilled out.

Brother and Sister took their money.

They ran out of the tree house.

Later, Mama saw the broken bank.

"Oh dear," said Mama.

"As Proverbs says, 'Cast but a glance at riches

and they are gone, for they will surely

sprout wings and fly off …'" she said.

"I hope they are using their

money wisely.

Just then, the door opened.

In came Brother and Sister.

They each had a huge lollipop.

"Cubs!" Mama said.

"You were saving for something special."

Mama did not see the small

box the cubs were hiding.

"We did, Mama," Sister said.

Mama said, "Lollipops are not special!"
She did not think Brother and Sister
had learned all about saving.

"We know," said Brother.
"But YOU are special, Mama,"
said Sister.
"Here is your birthday gift."

Mama said, "Oh dear!

It IS my birthday tomorrow.

May I open it now?"

"Yes!" said the cubs.

Mama's gift was a watch.

She was thankful to God

for her two loving cubs.

"What a fine gift," said Mama.

"Thank you.

But where did you get the lollipops?"

Brother said, "We got your watch
at Mr. Jones' store.
He gave them to us for being
such nice cubs."

"Mr. Jones is right about that.
You are nice cubs," said Mama.
"And like the Good Book says,
'their children will be a blessing.'"

And Mama gave Brother and Sister
a big bear hug.